W9-ATQ-246

OH YEAH!

by Tom Birdseye illustrated by Ethan Long

Holiday House / New York

To the annual
Real Guys Campout,
and its wacky spirit
of one-upmanship
T. B.

To Maurice Sendak,
and his wild things
E. L.

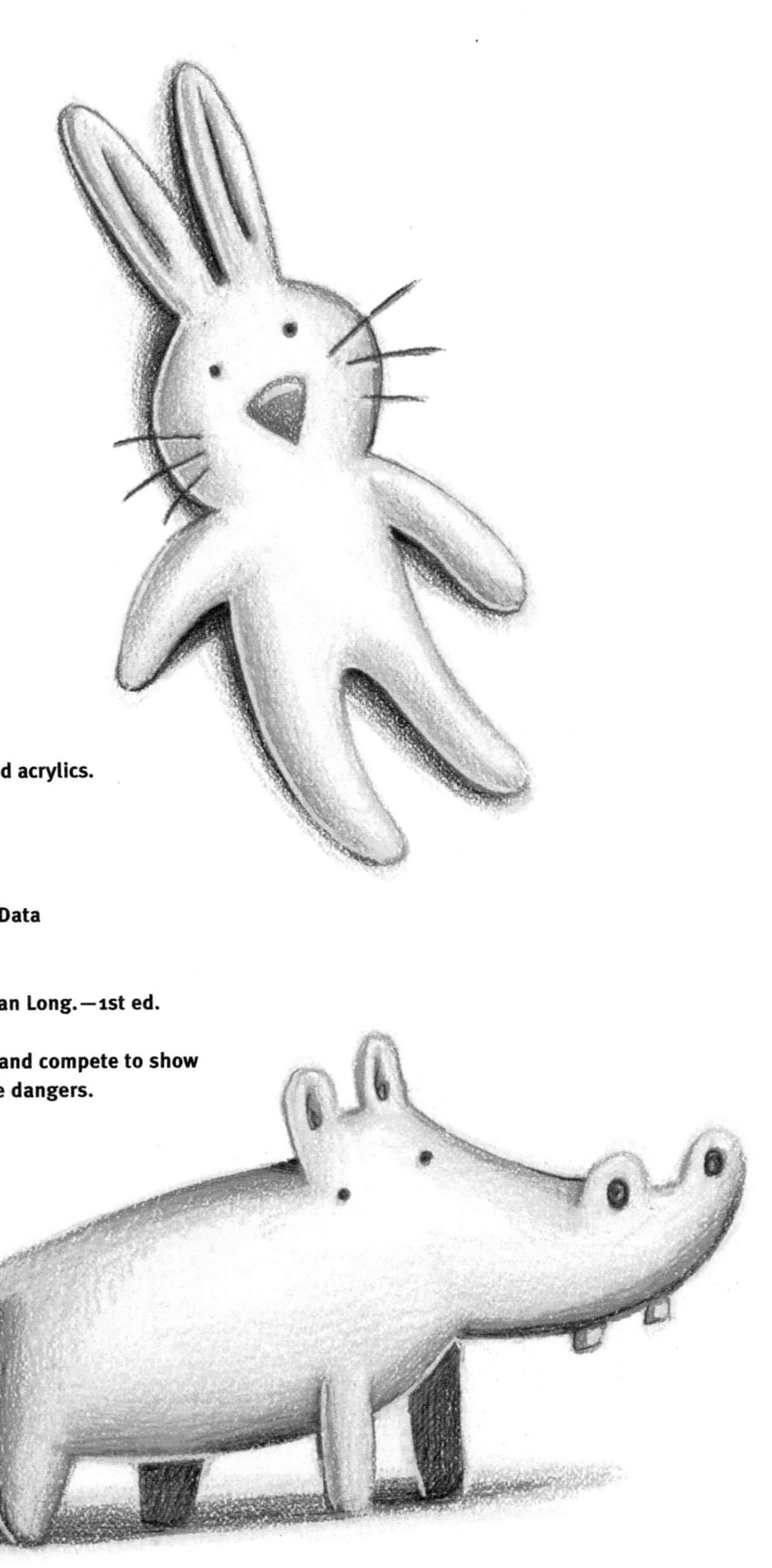

Printed in the United States of America
The text typeface is MetaPlus Bold.
The artwork was created using colored pencil and acrylics.
www.holidayhouse.com
First Edition

Library of Congress Cataloging-in-Publication Data

Birdseye, Tom.
Oh yeah! / by Tom Birdseye; illustrated by Ethan Long.—1st ed.
p. cm.
Summary: Two boys camp out in the backyard and compete to show their courage in the face of imagined nighttime dangers.
ISBN 0-8234-1649-6
[1. Courage—Fiction. 2. Camping—Fiction.]
I. Long, Ethan, ill. II. Title.

PZ7.B5213 Oh 2003
[E]—dc21
2002191319

Designed by Yvette Lenhart

One time my friend Jared and I camped out in the backyard.

"You're afraid of the dark," Jared said to me.

"Oh yeah?" I said.

Even though big, hairy, kid-eating monsters only come out at night,
I turned off my flashlight. "I could stay out here all night in the dark!"

But Jared looked me right in the eye and said, "Oh yeah?
I could stay out here all night in the dark even if. . .

. . .there were **spiders dangling over my head!"**

I frowned at Jared. Who's afraid of spiders? It's not like they're big, hairy, kid-eating monsters.

"Oh yeah?" I said. "I could stay out here all night in the dark even if there were spiders dangling over my head **and**. . .

. . . **snakes slithering around my feet!"**

Jared rolled his eyes.

"Oh yeah?" he said. "I could stay out here all night in the dark even if there were spiders dangling over my head, and snakes slithering around my feet, **and . . .**

...giant twenty-foot crocodiles crawling out of the fishpond!

I wouldn't be afraid! I'll show you!"

He grabbed his stuffed hippo, Norman, crawled out of the tent, and walked right up to the bank of the fishpond.

It was really dark over there by the fishpond, the perfect hiding place for big, hairy, kid-eating monsters.

But I said to Jared, "Oh yeah?"

I grabbed my stuffed rabbit, Alfred, and I walked right up to the bank of the fishpond too.

"I could stay out here all night in the dark," I said, "even if there were spiders dangling over my head, and snakes slithering around my feet, and giant twenty-foot crocodiles crawling out of the fishpond, **and** . . .

...saber-toothed tigers on the prowl.

Me and Alfred would just tell them all to go away!"

Jared scowled at me.

"Oh yeah?" he said. "I could stay out here all night in the dark even if there were spiders dangling over my head, and snakes slithering around my feet, and giant twenty-foot crocodiles crawling out of the fishpond, and saber-toothed tigers on the prowl. I'd tell them all to go away, **and . . .**

. . . *I'd do it* without *Norman!*"

Now I scowled. "Prove it!" I said.

Jared's eyebrows went up, and I figured he was probably worrying about big, hairy, kid-eating monsters.

But he took a deep breath and sat Norman down by the maple tree.

"Oh yeah?" I said to Jared. Even though the wind made the maple tree creak and groan, I wasn't worried about big, hairy, kid-eating monsters either. I took a deep breath, gave Alfred a hug, and set him down by the maple tree too.

"I could stay out here all night in the dark," I said, "even if there were spiders dangling over my head, and snakes slithering around my feet, and giant twenty-foot crocodiles crawling out of the fishpond, and saber-toothed tigers on the prowl, **and . . .**

. . . fire-breathing dragons
circling in the sky.
I'd punch them all in the nose.
So there!"

Just then there was a rustle and a thump in the bushes, and Jared and I both jumped. That rustle and thump sounded a lot like the kind of rustle and thump a big, hairy, kid-eating monster would make. Jared scooted closer to me.

"Oh yeah?" he said. "I could stay out here all night in the dark even if there were spiders dangling over my head, and snakes slithering around my feet, and giant twenty-foot crocodiles crawling out of the fishpond, and saber-toothed tigers on the prowl, and fire-breathing dragons circling in the sky, **and . . .**

. . . a big, hairy—"

The bushes shook.

Jared's voice shook too. "And a b-b-big, hairy, k-k-kid-eating . . ."

From the bushes came breathing—beastly, slobber-nosed breathing—exactly like a big, hairy, kid-eating monster's breath! The big, hairy, kid-eating monster breath drew closer . . .

and closer . . .

and closer.

Suddenly, out of the bushes lunged . . .

"A BIG, HAIRY, KID-EATING MONSTER!"

Jared and I both screamed.

We dove for the tent, crawled into our sleeping bags, and covered our eyes. Then I remembered.

“Alfred!”

He was still out there under the maple tree!

“Norman!” cried Jared.

What if the big, hairy, kid-eating monster liked to chomp on stuffed rabbits and hippos too?

In a flash we were back out in the dark, charging for the maple tree. “We’ll save you!” we shouted. “Get away, big, hairy, kid-eating monster, get away!”

And it did. That big, hairy, kid-eating monster gave a yelp and ran, looking kind of like . . . well, a lot like my dog, Merietta.

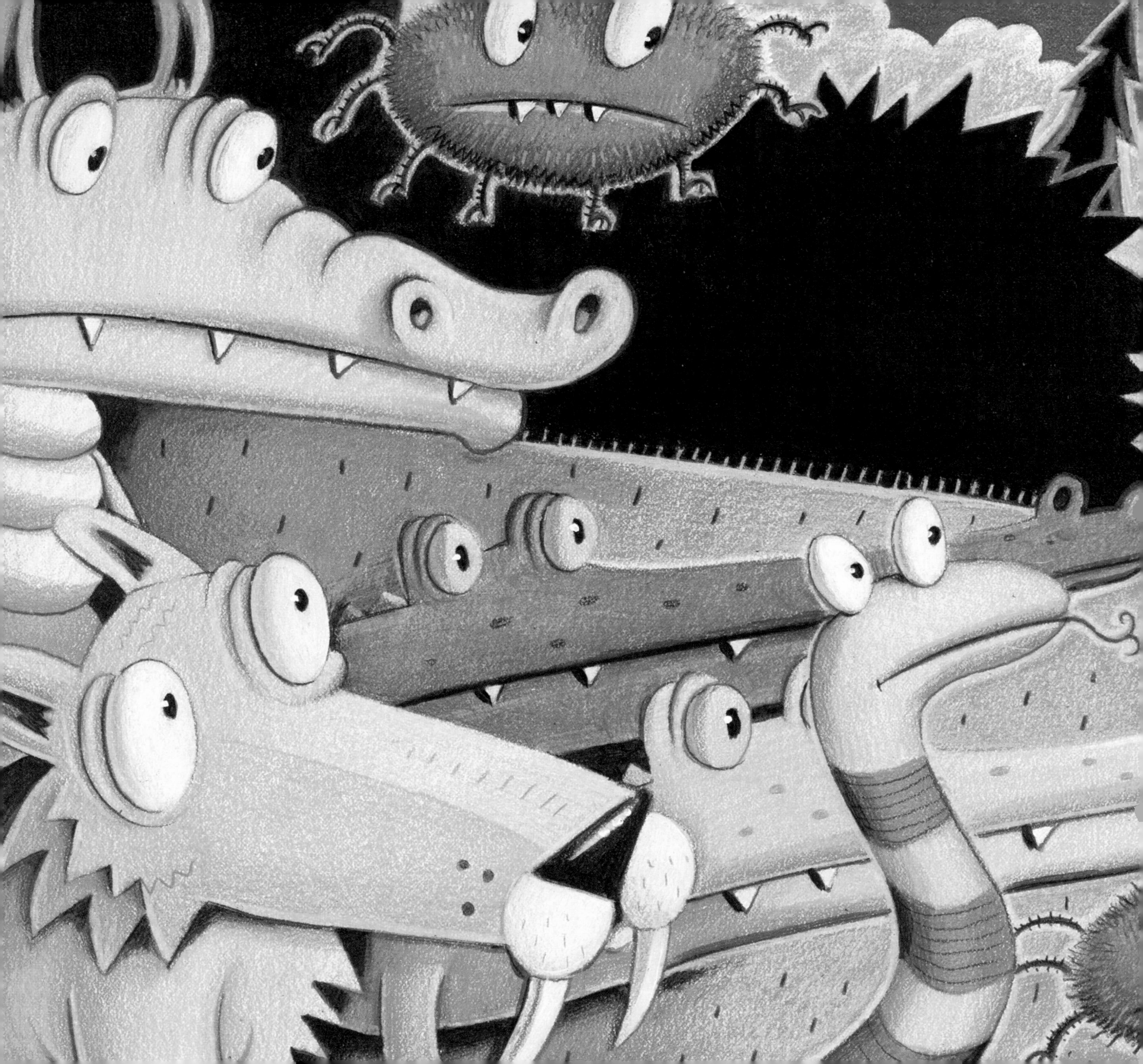

After my heart calmed down a little and my breath got back to normal, I whispered to Jared, "I wasn't scared."

"Me neither," said Jared. We scooped up Alfred and Norman and hurried back into the tent.

We turned on the
flashlight, just so we
could see each
other a little
better.
"We're both
really brave,"
said Jared.
I hugged Alfred
close
and said,
"Oh yeah?"

And someone said, "Yeah."